KIT AND MATEO
JOURNEY INTO THE CLOUDS

BY CARI MEISTER
ILLUSTRATED BY ADAM RECORD

 LEARNING ABOUT CLOUDS

PICTURE WINDOW BOOKS
a capstone imprint

Kit and Mateo looked up at the sky. A few fluffy white clouds slowly moved with the wind.

"Look, Jasper!" Kit said. "That cloud looks like you!"

Jasper purred and rubbed his head on Kit's leg.

"What are clouds anyway?" asked Mateo.

Kit shrugged. "I wish I knew."

Mateo started sketching. A sudden gust of wind ruffled the pages of his notebook. When Mateo looked up, he was face-to-face with a little cloud.

"Hello," said the cloud. "I heard you don't know much about me."

"WHOA!" said Mateo. "I must be dreaming."

Jasper let out a loud MEOW and jumped behind Kit.

SWOOSH!

Kit reached out and touched the little cloud. It felt wet and cold.

"You're not fluffy and dry like I thought you would be," she said.

"Do you know what clouds are made of?" asked the little cloud.

"I guess not," answered Kit.

"Let's find out," said the little cloud.

"Clouds are part of the water cycle," said the little cloud. "See that large puddle on the sidewalk?"

"Sure," answered Mateo.

"The sun is warming the water," said the little cloud. "As it warms, the water turns into vapor and rises to the sky. It's called evaporation."

SLURP!

"And let me guess," said Kit, "that makes clouds!"

"Eventually," said the little cloud. "But the water cycle doesn't stop there."

WATER CYCLE

There are almost 100 different kinds of clouds. But there are three main kinds: cirrus, cumulus, and stratus.

1. EVAPORATION

Jasper hopped onto the little cloud. Kit and Mateo followed.

"Up into the clouds we go!" said the little cloud. "You can't see the water vapor here, but it's cooling as it rises."

"So it's invisible?" asked Mateo.

"Yes, until it changes into water droplets or ice. That's called condensation," said the little cloud. "Take a closer look through this magnifying glass."

"I can see the droplets and ice sticking to particles in the air!" said Kit.

"Yes. When the droplets and ice clump together, they form a cloud," said the little cloud. "Now that you've seen a cloud forming, let's look at some clouds!"

Kit hugged Jasper tightly as they whizzed higher into the sky.

WATER CYCLE

3. CLOUD FORMATION

2. CONDENSATION

1. EVAPORATION

"The clouds here are long and feathery," said Kit.

"They're called cirrus clouds," said the little cloud.

"They look like long trails of white cotton candy," said Mateo.

"They look like cotton candy," said the little cloud, "but those clouds are made up of ice. If you lick ice, your tongue sticks to it! Let's move on."

Cirrus clouds form high in the sky where it is very cold. Because of this, they are made of ice crystals. They are found at heights of 20,000 feet (6,096 meters) or greater. Cirrus clouds are usually seen in fair weather.

A gust of wind blew the children and little cloud to another group of clouds.

"GIANT COTTON BALLS!" exclaimed Mateo.

"They're called cumulus clouds," said the little cloud.

"They're flat on the bottom and puffy on top," said Kit.

"JASPER! YOU CAN'T POUNCE ON A CLOUD!"

Kit said as she pulled Jasper into her lap.

MEOW!

Cumulus clouds are low clouds found mostly below 6,000 feet (1,829 meters). These clouds are usually found in fair weather.

"THAT WAS CLOSE!" said the little cloud.

"Now let's look at some clouds that aren't quite as nice."

"Do you know what kind of clouds these are?" asked the little cloud.

"We've already seen cirrus and cumulus," Mateo said. "These must be stratus clouds."

"Very good, Mateo!" said the little cloud.

"They look like gray blankets hanging low in the sky," said Kit.

Jasper yawned. Kit reached up and pulled one of the clouds closer to cover Jasper, but the cloud just made him wet.

"What's wrong, Jasper?" asked the cloud. "Don't you like water?"

"He needed a bath anyway!" said Mateo, giggling as he sketched in his notebook.

The little cloud blew the kids a bit farther south.

"The clouds here are really tall and wide, said

Mateo, "and they're dark."

SWOOSH!

"Right!" said the little cloud. They're cumulonimbus

clouds. They develop from cumulus clouds, and they

make thunderstorms."

Cumulonimbus clouds may reach 39,000 feet (11, 887 m) into the sky. These clouds can produce heavy rain and hail. They can also make lightning, strong winds, and even tornadoes.

BOOM!

FLASH!

CRASH!

Jasper hissed from Kit's lap. Then he backed down, shaking and quivering. "I know, Jasper!" said Kit. "Thunder and lightning can be scary!"

FLASH!

"When the cloud gets too heavy, the droplets and ice fall back to the earth. It's called precipitation, the fourth step of the water cycle," said the little cloud. And with that the little cloud drifted back down to the ground.

WATER CYCLE

3. CLOUD FORMATION

2. CONDENSATION

4. PRECIPITATION

1. EVAPORATION

"Last stop!" said the little cloud. "The final step of the water cycle happens when the water collects here on the ground. Then the cycle starts all over again."

"Thanks, little cloud," said Mateo, "Look at all the great sketches I drew."

"Your clouds are spectacular!" said the little cloud. "Bye. Look for me in the sky!"

"I had no idea cloud watching could be so fun," said Kit.

"Me neither," said Mateo.

Even Jasper had to agree, "MEOW!"

TAKE IT OUTSIDE!

Cloud watching is fun! Go outside and draw the clouds you see. Do the clouds look like animals? Cars? Castles? Use your imagination and have a great time!

What you need:

o paper

o pencil

o your imagination

GLOSSARY

cirrus cloud—a high, thin cloud made of ice crystals that looks like strands of white silk

condensation—changing from a gas to a liquid

cumulus cloud—a white, puffy cloud with a flat, rounded base

cumulonimbus cloud—a huge, tall cloud that can bring thunderstorms and tornadoes

crystal—a solid substance having a regular pattern and many flat surfaces

evaporation—changing from a liquid to a gas

precipitation—water that falls from the clouds in the form of rain, hail, or snow

particle—a tiny piece of something

stratus cloud—a low cloud that forms over a large area; stratus clouds often bring light rain

vapor—a gas made from a liquid

READ MORE

Edison, Erin. *Clouds.* Weather Basics. Mankato, Minn.: Capstone Press, 2012.

Lawrence, Ellen. *What Is the Water Cycle?* Weather Wise. New York: Bearport Pub., 2012.

Rockwell, Anne. *Clouds.* Let's-Read-and-Find-Out. Stage 1. New York: Collins, 2008.

INDEX

INTERNET SITES

FactHound offers a safe, fun way to find Internet sites related to this book. All of the sites on FactHound have been researched by our staff.

Here's all you do:

Visit www.facthound.com

Type in this code: 9781404883154

Super-cool stuff! Check out projects, games and lots more at www.capstonekids.com

Thanks to our advisers for their expertise, research, and advice:

Susan T. Lepri, PhD, Atmospheric and Space Sciences
University of Michigan

Terry Flaherty, PhD, Professor of English
Minnesota State University, Mankato

Editor: Shelly Lyons
Designer: Alison Thiele
Art Director: Nathan Gassman
Production Specialist: Jennifer Walker
The illustrations in this book were created digitally.

Picture Window Books are published by Capstone,
1710 Roe Crest Drive, North Mankato, Minnesota 56003
www.capstonepub.com

Library of Congress Cataloging-in-Publication Data
Meister, Cari.
Kit and Mateo journey into the clouds : learning about clouds / by Cari Meister ; illustrated by Adam Record.
p. cm. — (Take it outside)
"A Capstone imprint."
Summary: "Through the fantastical story of two young children, text and illustrations introduce the main kinds of clouds and the water cycle"— Provided by publisher.
Includes index.
ISBN 978-1-4048-8315-4 (library binding)
ISBN 978-1-4795-1936-1 (paperback)
ISBN 978-1-4795-1901-9 (ebook pdf)
1. Clouds—Juvenile literature. I. Record, Adam, ill. II. Title.
QC921.35.M45 2014
551.57'6—dc23   2013006272

Printed in the United States of America in
Stevens Point, Wisconsin.
032013   007227WZF13

LOOK FOR ALL THE BOOKS IN THE TAKE IT OUTSIDE SERIES:

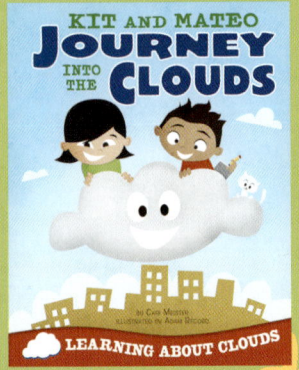

KIT AND MATEO JOURNEY INTO THE CLOUDS — LEARNING ABOUT CLOUDS

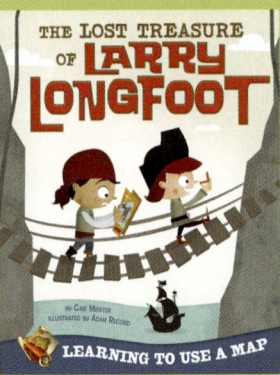

THE LOST TREASURE OF LARRY LONGFOOT — LEARNING TO USE A MAP

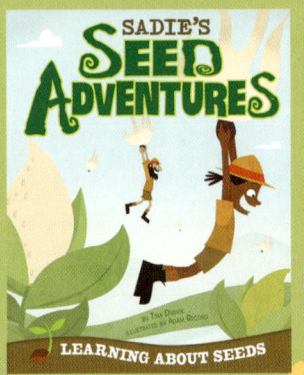

SADIE'S SEED ADVENTURES — LEARNING ABOUT SEEDS

SPACE COWBOY CALEB AND THE NIGHT SKY ROUND-UP — LEARNING ABOUT THE NIGHT SKY